Hill-Pehle Publishing

www.lulu.com/hillpehle

2012

Surviving in Post America

by

Dick Browning

ISBN 978-1-105-73206-5

Surviving In Post America

by

Dick Browning

ISBN 978-1-105-73206-5

CHAPTER ONE

Washington continued practicing massive deficit spending expanding social programs and mandating the various states do the same. Many state budgets tanked under the strain and were forced to seek federal bailouts. Individual wages fell tax revenues shrank. Employers laid off workers as the economy collapsed putting further strains on state budgets in unemployment pay. A scared population stocked up on gold, guns, and ammunition. Private debt grew to insane levels. The Federal Reserve printed more dollars backed by nothing. Foreign capitol fled the country. The government bailed out financial institutions holding shaky real-estate loans gone bad. Those who caused the crisis were in charge of fixing it. Someone described it as "the inmates running the asylum." The administration and congress continued proposing laws detrimental to a vibrant economy. OPEC no longer accepted the worthless U. S. dollar as payment for oil. The environmentalists blocked new drilling domestically by endless law suits.

Over a million citizens marched on Washington demonstrating for lower taxes and no new spending. The state controlled news media refused to acknowledge the magnitude of discontent exhibited. The New York Times reluctantly reported the march on page twenty three, estimating the crowd at "a few thousand."

Some rebellious Texans demanded a referendum for secession from the union.

Talk radio so effectively exposed corruption at every level of government, the population lost confidence in their elected leaders. Washington reacted by silencing all opposing voices. Freedom of the press and freedom of speech would not be tolerated as the nation descended toward totalitarian rule.

Many lost their fortunes in the first crash of the stock market. Investors pulled out. As things began to look better they got back in only to get hit harder in a next devastating sell-off.

In the first great depression in the nineteen thirties, Roosevelt made the ownership of gold illegal. People were required to swap their gold for paper money at a low rate. Once this was done, the president by executive order raised the price of gold substantially. Thus he wiped out much government debt. The majority of the population lost everything. Washington considered doing it again.

Rolling blackouts plagued the land. Air controllers, demanding a living wage, walked off their jobs curtailing air travel. Goods and services were unreliable. Rampant inflation put grocery prices out of reach for many. Those with jobs were paid ever increasing amounts for their work. Out of work and retired people on fixed incomes could no longer afford much of anything. Government run soup kitchens opened in the cities. Those too proud to accept charity starved.

Eventually angry mobs descended on the capitol killing lawmakers. The president fled to an undisclosed location. Senators and representatives cowered in secret hiding places fearing for their lives. Washington resembled scenes reminiscent of the bloody French Revolution. Federal control evaporated into chaos. States struggled to compensate, trying to regain responsibilities long since ceded to Washington.

In Dallas, Fred and Helen Harvey played by the rules. They worked hard and built up a sizable nest-egg in their 401K retirement fund only to have it decimated in the stock market. Now Washington expected Americans to bail out those who lived irresponsibly. The Harveys sold what was left of their stocks only to have inflation make the money worthless. Then Fred lost his job.

Now it was September, time for sixteen year old Josh to return to school, but the streets were too unsafe to attend school. A stretched city budget could not provide security for its citizens. Roving bands of hungry thugs roamed freely, looting and killing.

At nine thirty one evening, the lights went out across Dallas. It was clearly time to flee, but where? Helen suggested south to the coast, a warmer place to spend the winter. Anywhere appeared safer than the city.

Anticipating the possibility of needing to leave in a hurry, Fred had packed a chest of food, water, and emergency supplies as recommended by FEMA.

Forty one year old Fred felt the burdens of the world on his shoulders. How was he going to provide for Helen and Josh? He was a computer programmer in a world unplugged from electricity. Slight of build and with thinning hair, he was never much of an outdoors man. What was he going to do on the coast or anywhere else?

He put the chest containing the emergency supplies in the trunk of the little Toyota. Anticipating trouble, he had armed himself with a pistol and shotgun, but never became proficient with them. He put both and three boxes of shells on the floor of the back seat. Birth certificates, passports, marriage license and other important papers along with their three gold coins were placed beneath the driver's seat in a water-proof folder.

Helen, three years younger than Fred, wore her long homey blond curls cascading down her shoulders. Her hair was the envy of her fellow nurses at the hospital, but in times of stress like the present, it was a bother to maintain. Keeping her trim figure was increasingly more difficult as the years passed. Now being pretty and slender was the least of her worries. She worried about getting enough to eat.

She mourned the loss of their possessions, all they had scraped and saved to accumulate. Flashlight in hand, she took one last look around the house to see what else they should take. She grabbed pillows, blanket, and clothes. The rest would have to stay behind; the furniture, the computer, the appliances, everything they owned and the house with its mortgage. Grieving wouldn't help. "Come on, Josh, let's get in the car."

Fred was right behind them. He started to lock the house. What is the use? Looters would just break down the door. Maybe he, Helen, and Josh would return. Who knows?

Sixteen year old Josh took his computer games. He had become a bit of a couch potato. One might call him pudgy. Gym class instructors let the students walk around the grounds. The boy shunned demanding exercise. Wherever the family was going, he hoped there would be good television. At least this outing would be a break from the old routine, an extension of summer vacation.

Outside it was dark, no street lights. Fred heard gunfire in the distance. He backed the car out of the driveway and headed south toward Interstate 45.

Before they motored a mile, they encountered an angry mob of men blocking the street. Some carried guns, others wielded ball bats. They signaled for Fred to stop, but he knew he must not. He leaned on the horn. Most men backed away, but one stood defiantly in his path.

Fred slowed to a crawl and sounded the horn again. One of the men bashed in Helen's window with the butt of his rifle.

Fred gunned the motor and drove over the man who blocked his way.

"Look out!" shouted Helen. "I think you killed that man!"

Setting his jaw, Fred shrugged. "It was either him or us. He wouldn't get out of the way." Still, it bothered him. He felt remorse. What had he done? Did he do the right thing?

As they sped off, the crowd gathered around their fallen comrade. Their leader, the one they called Hammer, wrote down Fred's license number. "The bastard killed my brother. I'll track him down and see he dies slowly."

Fred made a quick left turn, went a few blocks and turned again when he saw others in the street ahead. Now he was in an unfamiliar neighborhood. He became disoriented and didn't know which direction he was going. Street signs were impossible to read with no lights. At length, he decided it was foolish to continue. For all he knew he was going away from the south exit to the city. They were in a residential neighborhood. Fred turned up an alley and into a drive to someone's garage. He killed the engine and lights. "We will just stay here till morning unless someone runs us off. I can't navigate in the dark."

Helen and Josh eventually drifted off to sleep. Fred could not. All night long he sat in the driver's seat thinking of the man he ran over and pondering what he should do.

At first light, he started off again. Getting his bearings, he headed for I-45 and the Texas coast. Their troubles were just beginning. A mass exodus of Dallas turned Interstate-45 into a 300 mile long parking lot. The pace was maddening, stop and go. Texas summer had not given up. The temperature hovered around a hundred. Nerves were frayed and people on the road were testy.

Josh asked to pull off the highway so he could pee. "No way, Josh, I'm afraid no one would let us back in line. Go in a paper cup and pour it out the window." Helen had a real problem peeing in a paper cup when she tried it.

They got a better idea of the problem of losing one's place in line when Fred stopped to let two ladies in an old Ford back on the highway in front of him. The ladies had stopped at a service station. The Rage filled man behind them honked his horn. When that didn't work, he tried to push Fred's car to fill the gap so the women could not get in. The man backed off when Fred grabbed his shotgun and aimed it out the window at him.

There was one long wait where no one was moving. They had not eaten since leaving home. Fred got out of the car and retrieved the emergency chest and put it in the back seat with Josh. One of the ladies from the car in front got out and walked back to talk to Fred and Helen. The line began to creep forward and Fred told her to get in.

She crowded in the back with Josh and the chest. "Have you got any water?" she asked. "My friend is about to pass out. We stopped back there where you let us back on the road, but they were out of everything." She dabbed her face with a paper towel. "With no electricity, the ice machine didn't work. They had gas, but couldn't pump it. We couldn't buy so much as a Twinkie. Two men got in an argument over the last fried pie and one pulled a gun on the other. These people are animals. What's happening to us?"

Helen gave the woman a gallon milk jug filled with water. The next time the line of cars stopped, the lady got out and returned to her own vehicle.

And so it went as hour after frustrating hour crept by. To save gas, Fred would not use the car's air conditioner. When the heat got unbearable, he would turn the cool air on for a few minutes. It didn't cool the car down much since the mob had broken out Helen's window the night before.

Josh complained bitterly about the heat, the traffic, and everything in general. Fred considered his son. He was cute when he was younger, but now in his teens, he showed no promise at all. Would he ever grow up?

To add to the misery, WBAP radio out of Dallas. Reported a hurricane was approaching the Texas coast. Evacuating to the coast seemed a good idea last night, but not now.

` Nearing Corsicana, they began to see large numbers of cars coming the other way from Houston. It was obvious the coast was no safer than Dallas. They no longer had enough fuel to make it that far anyway. Fred opted to pull off the interstate and head east on highway 31. Perhaps they could find gas in some little town. Maybe they could make better time on the country roads. He was right about making better time. But no service stations were pumping gas. Josh thought it was so much better anyway. They were moving. It felt like they were getting some place and there was some air moving through the car.

Arriving at Athens, Texas, there was a line of cars backed up on the highway. A policeman walked up. "There is no place for you to stay here. We have taken in all the refugees we can handle. It is stretching our resources. I will escort you and all of these cars to the edge of town and you will have to go someplace else."

Leaving Athens, Fred reached his limit of endurance. It was getting dark, time to look for a place to camp out. Maybe things would look more hopeful tomorrow. He pulled off the highway onto a narrow county road. When he came upon a dirt drive heading back into some trees, he took it. They had enough food for a few days. Josh always liked camping. Fred wondered how he would like it on a permanent basis. What would they do when the food and water ran out? Fred had all the challenges he could handle for one day. He would not think about what next, not tonight anyway. He marveled at Helen. What a strong woman. She sat there, looking serene, facing another night of sleeping in the car.

When they stopped under a tree, Josh pulled the survival chest out of the back seat of the Toyota giving him room to lie down for the night. It started to rain.

Helen got the flashlight and rummaged through the chest in the rain. Then she snapped. "What is it with those FEMA people? In their recommended list, they tell us to bring a can opener when we have no cans to open. We should pack a medicine dropper. What for? We packed matches when the wood is too wet to burn. But they didn't think to mention that it might be nice if we brought along a God damn roll of toilet paper!"

Fred marveled. Helen wasn't coping as well as he thought. He never heard her swear before. She had obviously reached her limit.

CHAPTER TWO

Early next morning Fred, Helen, and Josh were awakened by someone beating on the hood of the car. "Hey in there. You are on private property. Go find a public park some place."

Fred lowered his window to face an older man wearing boots, jeans and a ball cap. The rain had stopped and the sun reflected off beads of water all around, making every surface appear to be covered by sparkling jewels. The fresh country air smelled delicious.

"Good morning, sir," said Fred. "We came in last night in the rain lost and out of gas and not knowing where to go. I take it we are trespassing on your land. You must be Mister Larson of El Rancho. I saw the name on the mail box as we pulled in."

"That's right, Dick Larson. You can't stay here. Move on down the road."

Helen's eyes filled with tears. "Just where are we supposed to go?" she sobbed. "They wouldn't let us stop in Athens. No place to eat, no motel rooms, no place to take a shower. What kind of people are you around here? We are Texans. Texans are supposed to be friendly." She broke down and cried uncontrollably.

Larson couldn't deal with a crying woman. It completely unnerved him. He changed his tune. "Er, ah, now, don't cry ma'am. Oh hell, follow me down to the house and have a cup of coffee."

They followed Larson's pickup down the poorly maintained dirt drive. Josh figured the house would be some un-kept shack. He was surprised when they pulled up in front of a mound of earth with well-maintained grounds. Steps led down into the earth sheltered house.

Larson stepped down out of his pickup and invited them to follow him inside. They descended the steps, entered the door at the bottom and found themselves in a large living area furnished in Texas ranch style. A clock in the shape of a cow skull hung on a wall. A cow hide covered the couch. Long horns hung over the door and a Remington bronze statuette graced the coffee table. The house was sunk into the side of a hill. To the left, windows looked out over a spacious back yard flanked by trees and sloping to a lake thirty yards down the hill. A heavy Mexican dining table with four chairs stood in front of them. To the right was the kitchen separated from the family room by a counter.

"Hey, Honey, we've got company," Larson called out.

Mrs. Larson appeared from down a connecting hall. She was gray haired, short and frail with a motherly caring air about her.

"I found these three parked down in front under a tree," said Larson. "They accused me of being unfriendly when I beat on their car and told them to move on. Just too sensitive, I reckon."

Fred stepped forward. "I'm Fred Harvey, Mrs. Larson. This is my wife and son, Helen and Josh. We just drove down from Dallas. Now we are out of gas and I'm afraid we're stranded."

"I'm Joyce," she said. Gesturing toward the table, "Please sit down. Would you like some pie and coffee? Dick, fetch another chair for the boy."

Larson disappeared down another hall and came back with a chair.

"What an interesting house you have here," said Fred as they took their seats. "I've heard of earth sheltered houses, but never saw one."

"I built it myself," said Larson. "Had it designed by a firm up in Oklahoma. The banks wouldn't finance it, so I said to hell with 'em, I'll build it out of pocket. We put a mobile home up on the hill there to live in and got an earth mover to scrape out the side of the hill. By the time we got the walls up and eleven inches of solid concrete roof on it, I had five miles of steel in it and two hundred twenty tons of concrete in the shell. I was out of money and had to stop building."

Helen could hold her discomfort no longer. "Mrs. Larson. I hate to impose but can I use your restroom?"

"Certainly, dear," said Joyce. "It is right down that hall on the right."

"I was making good money at the time," Larson continued, "but taxes were eating us up. I kept saying, 'I need a tax break.' That old mobile home had lousy insulation. We couldn't keep it cool in the summer. Joyce kept saying 'I will not live another summer in this mobile home.'"

Helen returned to the table just as Joyce brought in a tray of coffee and pie. "Do you drink coffee, Josh?"

"No, ma'am. Do you have any milk?"

"Afraid not, son. The grocery stores have shut down in town and we don't have a cow."

Larson continued with his story. "So, anyway, I kept saying I needed a tax break and Joyce kept repeating she would not live another summer in that mobile home. Then along came a tornado and blew the mobile home away with us in it. We saw it coming and jumped in the bath tub. When it was all over, we were still in the tub, but it was lying on its side on the ground. We found the bath tub at the other end of the mobile home a mile away in a tree. We just got in the right bath tub. Joyce and I stood up and walked away unharmed. People told us how lucky we were, but I say if we had any luck at all, we wouldn't have been hit by a tornado. Of course that is not altogether true. Joyce didn't have to live another summer in the mobile home, I got my tax break and insurance money from the destroyed mobile home allowed us to resume building. I believe when you keep emotionally affirming something like 'I need a tax break,' and 'I will not live another summer in that mobile home,' it is the same as a prayer. Something happens. Eight weeks later we moved into the unfinished shell. Joyce was cooking with an electric skillet on the kitchen floor there. We built around ourselves for years." Larson looked at his guests. "We named our place 'El Rancho.' That is close to all the Spanish I know. It isn't much of a ranch, only fifty acres."

Meanwhile, Joyce served the pie and coffee and took her seat at the table. "Tell me, Mr. Harvey, how you happened to end up stranded here?"

Fred launched into a long tale of their adventures of the past couple of days ending with, "And here we are, out of gas and not knowing where to turn."

Larson pulled his chair closer to the table. "We moved out of Dallas thirty years ago. What took you so long to figure it out? It would take wild horses to drag us back, especially now with all this trouble. A person would be crazy to live in the city."

Fred shook his head. "Mr. Larson, we don't want to be a burden. If you can help us get some gas, we will move on."

"It may not be that easy. Out here in the country, we are all holding on to what we have for fear there won't be any more. The power company is shut down. We're running on solar generated power. I doubt they have electricity in town. With no electricity, no gasoline can be pumped. I guess you folks can stay till we figure out how to get you on your way. Don't want you trashing the place out though, and we can't feed you. We've got a little food stashed away for us, but not for all the hungry refugees from the city that might stop by."

Josh looked out the window. "I see a lake down there. Are there fish in it? "

Larson nodded. "There sure are. Come back around three this afternoon. We will go catch some."

"We can't let these people just sit out there in their car, Dick," said Joyce. "I see no reason they can't bed down in the stable. It isn't being used."

When they finished their coffee Larson suggested he show the way to the horse barn.

"You go ahead", said Helen. "I will help Mrs. Larson with the dishes. I can walk up. It isn't far. I saw it on the way down here. The walk will do me good."

The Harveys settled into the stable. There was a place to park the car in the breezeway down the center. Horse stalls were on either side. Fred spread fresh hay in one of the stalls and put a horse blanket on top for a bed for him and Helen. In another stall he did the same for Josh. There was even a toilet and wash basin in a little water closet.

The Larson's El Rancho consisted of fifty acres. But only twenty acres were cleared. The rest was heavily wooded. Josh had scavenged fire wood from beneath the trees, but it was too wet to burn. On clear nights they could build a fire outside. It wasn't exactly Motel Six, but better than sleeping in the car.

Fred pondered their situation. So we stay here till we can get gas. How long will that be? Will we starve in the meantime? We only packed a dozen MRE's (military meals ready to eat) and a jar of peanut butter. Then what? Where can we go? Will the Gulf coast be any better?

Indeed, the coast was not any better. A million homeless people milled about looking for food and shelter. Unsanitary conditions were already making people sick. A worldwide depression was setting in bringing with it poverty, pestilence, and all manner of human suffering.

CHAPTER 3

At three o'clock, Josh walked down to the house to go fishing. Larson gathered up rods, reels, tackle boxes, and paddles, then they walked down to the water. The lake was only seven acres and an easy paddle to anywhere they wanted to go. There was a little aluminum row boat kept upside down in the back yard so it didn't fill with water when it rained. They turned it right side up, launched it, and got aboard.

"We put this lake in when we first moved onto the place," explained Larson. "Stocked it with bass, crappy, catfish and perch. The perch are to feed the bass, but they tend to reproduce too fast. The big perch compete with the bass for food and eat the bass and catfish eggs. Perch are good eating, if you can get around the bones. We catch and eat a lot of perch to keep the population down. They are the tastiest eating and easiest to catch." He pointed to a pile of brush breaking the surface out in the middle of the lake. "Let's paddle over there."

When they got there, Larson tied up to a tree limb sticking out of the water. "Here is the best crappie fishing," he said. "The crappie like to hide in among the brush then dash out to eat a small perch, bug or whatever strikes their fancy." He held up a small lure. "This usually attracts them. He attached it to Josh's line and told him where to cast it. Almost immediately Josh got a strike and reeled in a nice crappie. It was speckled and looked like something between a very large perch and a small bass.

Josh was impressed. His dad was always too busy to take him fishing. He never had anyone who knew what he was doing take him fishing. After they caught several crappy, Larson took Josh to another location and explained what lure was best for bass. They soon reeled in two five pounders.

Larson enjoyed teaching the boy. The grandson he had hoped for never happened. "The catfish are something else again," he explained. "We stocked channel catfish but there are also some mud cats that seemed to come from out of nowhere. They are all good to eat. I throw out a commercial catfish food for them. Or at least I did when I could still get it. It is roughly the same formulae as dog food and it floats till it gets water logged.

The Aggies, that's experts from Texas A & M University, hold conferences on commercially raising catfish. They advise getting little fingerlings in the spring from a commercial fish hatchery and feed them till fall then harvest them. For every pound and a half of catfish food you throw out, you can expect a pound of catfish. That is efficient. You can't expect protein production like that from any other farm animal. Commercially raised channel catfish are a big farm crop here in Texas and also in Mississippi, Louisiana, and Arkansas."

Josh was not interested in catfish. He was ready to stick with the excitement of bringing in more fighting bass and crappie. Larson could tell he wasn't paying attention. He put his hand on Josh's shoulder to get his full attention. His tone became serious. "Josh, I said in the beginning I wasn't going to feed you and your family. Until we find gas to get you on your way, you will need to learn all you can about getting food, any kind of food to keep you alive. That goes for either here or anywhere you go for that matter. I tell you, this nation is in bad trouble and many will starve because they don't know how to forage for food. You best pay attention about the catfish, too. They could make the difference. I usually put out a trot line for the catfish. I'll show you how this evening, if you like."

Larson began to paddle back toward the house. He continued his tale about catfish raishttp://www.techprotectbags.comhttp://www.techprotectbags.coming. "The private fish hatcheries will be shut down now. No more buying the little fingerlings. The catfish will reproduce on their own if you give them shelter where they can hatch their eggs and protect their young without the other fish coming in and eating them. I made a couple of brooders for catfish as described by a local fish hatchery. You take two five gallon buckets and fasten them together at the open ends. Then make a hole just big enough for an adult catfish to enter in one end. Put some concrete inside along the length of the two buckets so the brooder will stay on the bottom. Place the brooder with the open end facing toward the center of the lake in water deep enough it will still be underwater during the dry season."

By this time they had caught all the fish they could eat. Without refrigeration, fish would quickly spoil. Larson continued his dialogue on fishing. "As I was saying, I throw out a commercial catfish food for the catfish, but the perch found out they like it too. They are so voracious about it the catfish stopped coming up." Larson was in the front of the boat. He dug in the paddle and pointed the bow toward the shore. "When the food hits the water, the surface explodes with gorging perch. But I need to thin out the perch population anyway. I've taken to using a throw net. I feed the food to the fish every morning. Then about once a week I throw the casting net on top of the feeding perch. Sometimes I can catch as many at thirty in one cast. The big ones I clean, the ones small enough for the bass to eat, I throw back. Come to the pier tomorrow morning about seven and I will show you how."

Larson sighed. "I still have some catfish food; I guess I won't be able to get any more."

Back at the yard, they pulled the boat up on shore, turned it over, and took their catch to the pier where there was a counter for cleaning. Larson demonstrated his cleaning, filleting, and skinning technique and then instructed Josh to do the rest while he gave pointers.

"Now, I'm not just teaching you this for fun," said Larson. "From now on you fish on the halves. You will be fishing to feed both your family and mine."

Josh came away from the fishing experience a different person. It was something like a rite of passage to becoming a man. He had taken his first lesson in providing for the family. He learned things even his dad did not know. It could be on his shoulders to keep the family alive. He walked a little straighter. He would put away childish video games and view his role in society in a new light.

Joyce invited the Harvey family for a fish fry that evening.

When Josh and his family returned to the stable, Josh was excited. "Mr. Larson used to teach survival skills in the Navy," Josh said. "He said he would teach me how to survive on this place like the Indians did. Why do we have to go someplace else? Will we be any better off?"

"We are uninvited guests here," said his mother. "I don't know how long we will be welcome. It will be up to us to be the best guests possible. Keep an eye out to be helpful whenever possible. The Larsons are elderly. They can use all the help we can give them. I plan the help Mrs. Larson as much as she will let me, and your dad will do the same for Mr. Larson. Maybe we can be so useful they won't want to let us go."

Chapter 4

A special bond grew between Larson and the boy. Josh was such an eager student of Larson's survival lore. The day after the fishing trip, Larson took him into the woods and pointed out which plants were edible, which were poisonous, and which had healing properties.

"How can you tell if a plant is poison?" asked Josh.

They sat down on a fallen log. "Good question," said Larson.

"The Department of the Army publishes a book titled THE COMPLETE GUIDE TO EDIBLE WILD PLANTS. In it, gives a test to make sure a plant is not poisonous. I have a copy of that back at the house. Remind me. I will loan it to you. "

The fall color was coming on. Oaks were dropping their acorns. "I suppose your family can survive on just fish," said Larson, "but you will get tired of it. The Indians who preceded us on this land relied on acorns to sustain them over the winter. An acre of oaks can provide as much nutrition in acorns as an acre of corn. "

Josh picked up an acorn and peeled the hull and tasted it. It was bitter and he shook his head.

"I know it is bitter," said the old man. "That is because it is full of tannin. Once you leach out the tannin it is edible. When we get back from our walk, I suggest you and your folks get some buckets from the stable and come back out here and gather all the acorns you can before the leaves fall and you can't find them anymore. Hull them, crush them, and leach them out in water until the water doesn't turn brown any more. You want to get enough to last all winter. It takes three cups of acorns to make one cup of acorn flour."

There were some late season flowers blooming in a clearing. Honey bees were working the blossoms. "You like honey?" asked Larson.

"Sure," said Josh.

"See if you can follow those bees back to their hive. It will be full of honey. Chances are it is an old hollow tree. We can come back tomorrow and harvest buckets of glorious sweetness."

It wasn't easy to follow a honey bee. Josh would lose sight of one then he would see another heading in the same general direction. They led him to their home.

"All those worker bees are female," said Larson as he followed a few minutes later. "The queen is female as well. The only males are a few drones who do no work at all. One mates with the queen on her maiden flight. Then she returns to the hive and spends the rest of her life laying thousands of eggs that are cared for till they mature into worker bees. Honey It is a good substitute for sugar and is good for curing allergies. Don't plan on getting rich raising bees to sell the honey though. Foreign suppliers keep the price of honey low. I guess foreign bees must work for less money."

Just as Larson had predicted, the bees were entering and leaving a hole in a large old oak tree. The hole was several feet above their heads.

"Come winter, the drones, having served their purpose, are shut out of the hive and left to die," Continued Larson. "It reminds me of the feminist movement. Since we have mechanized everything, hard physical labor is mostly a thing of the past. Men are no longer needed to hunt game for the tribe. Even warfare has been feminized. We have lady fighter pilots and women aboard ship. It wasn't that way when I was in the Navy."

They started walking back to the house and Larson continued his rant about the difference between men and women. "Guys are different from the girls. Since all this feminism stuff started, I hear the ladies fault us for our differences. Women revel in man bashing. We won't stop to ask directions. We want command of the TV remote control. For us, the remote isn't to change channels; it is to continually channel surf to see what else is on. They complain all we want to do is drink beer and watch football.

"When the annual Darwin Awards come out, it is always the guys listed doing stupid things. We put JATO bottles on our Chevy to see how fast it will go. We snow board over cliffs and go swimming with sharks on a dare. I hear these women making fun of us and eyeing us like drones as useful for breeding purposes, but not much good for anything else.

"When I get flak from the girls, I explain men to them this way. Men are made for the outside. We were designed that way. For thousands of years, it was the men who defended the tribe and went out to hunt wild beasts for food while the women stayed in the cave to tend the hearth and mind the children. The survival of the race depended on the willingness, even need, of men to face danger. It takes a certain mentality to go out with your buddies armed with nothing but spears to take down a full grown bull mastodon. It is like I tell the women, "You may make fun of us now, but you will feel different when the mastodons come back."

Larson realized he had strayed from the lesson on gathering honey. He continued. "I used to raise honey bees to pollinate my berry crop. I still have some of the old hive boxes out in the barn. We will get the whole bee colony in a hive and set it up close to the house where we don't have to look for a bee tree to harvest honey in the future."

Helen had been right about the Larsons needing help. Life had become almost too much for Joyce to handle. They needed a helping hand. Fred would have been bored just sitting around. He enjoyed working with Larson, feeding the chickens, tilling the plot for a fall garden, mowing and raking up leaves. At their first encounter he had thought Larson was a grouchy old man, but once they were invited to stay, Larson had mellowed. He enjoyed having Fred around to help out and listen to his endless stories. Over the years small incidents had been embellished to where they were epic comedies. Getting on in years, Larson would sometimes tell the same story over again. Fred would listen attentively each time and laugh at the appropriate times.

Joyce and Helen clicked from the start. Joyce had been lonely before Helen came. Not that she and Dick didn't get along; they had a good marriage, but Larson was no good at girl talk. Helen and Joyce would sit at the table over a cup of coffee and talk every morning. And after the lunch nap they shared in cleaning and cooking. It became a joy rather than a burden. Joyce was not looking forward to the day when Fred and Helen would continue on their way.

CHAPTER FIVE

A Dallas, hospital filled with the injured from street violence.

When the electricity went out, water and sewer services broke down. Garbage pickup ceased. The lack of sanitation and ability to procure drugs, precipitated Cholera, Bubonic plague, leprosy, and other diseases. Thousands needed hospitalization. Overworked staff struggled to render aid, but eventually refused to admit further patients. As food and medicine ran out, the ailing were sent home. There was little that could be done for them.

The dead piled up. The stench was unbearable. An armed "body squad" patrolled the city, bringing the dead to a central location for burial in mass graves. Looters caught robbing the corpses were shot and collected with the rest for interment. Three men were assigned to write down the names of the dead where possible. If there was no identification on the body, tattoos and, scars, birth marks, and approximate age were noted in hopes surviving relatives might later be able to track the fate of their loved ones. The three men were fitted with orange vests to identify them lest they be mistaken as looters and shot. The task became too great. They asked for help, but no one volunteered. Overwhelmed, they gave up the task and went home to look after their families.

A bulldozer worked day and night burying corpses.

Eventually, the hospital staff gave up the fight. One by one or sometimes in bunches they simply walked away.

Then there was only nurse, fifty year old Betty Andrews attending to the needs of patients with no home to return to and those too sick or near death to move. She refused to quit. Betty was the stuff saints are made of, a totally loving, caring, giving woman. Though scarcely more than skin and bones, alone, she moved the sick to one ward where she could better attend to their needs.

Betty worked tirelessly except for her quiet hour at the beginning of the day when she communed with spirit. "I take this presence with me for the rest of the day." She mused. "It guides, comforts, and sustains me."

Sometimes when exhaustion overtook, she curled up on an empty bed and slept In short naps. When food ran out in the kitchen, she raided personnel refrigerators the staff had stocked for their own lunches and snacks. She lovingly brought this food to her patients.

The street gang led by Hammer, altered tactics to adjust to the new reality. The dollar was no more. With no money, drugs and prostitution were no longer profitable. Businesses shut down and revenue from protection rackets dried up. One night, Hammer commandeered a tanker truck and led his men to the hospital. An electric generator supplied emergency power to the facility. Its diesel fuel would be easy to steal. While they were at it, four of his men were sent inside to the pharmacy to search for narcotics.

When Betty heard the commotion, she went to investigate. She found four thieves in the pharmacy. Seeing what they were up to, she stood in the doorway and ordered them out. "Surely you can see this place is for tending the sick and dying. You have no business here."

"Shut up, you bossy broad. We run this town now," said the one with the red beard. "I haven't gotten laid all day. I believe I'll have a piece of you." He advanced toward her.

She held her ground in defiance, but the bluff didn't work. Red was determined to carry out his threat. "Come on guys. Help me catch her."

Betty slammed the door, dashed down a hallway, and into a stairwell. A rush of adrenalin propelled her up the stairs faster than she had ever run before.

Red and his buddies were not far behind laughing at the sport of the chase.

Suddenly, the power went out to the building as the emergency generator, starved of fuel, sputtered to a halt.

Exiting into a hallway on the floor above, Betty had some advantage as she was familiar with the darkened building. Unfortunately she was running up a hall with rooms on both sides but no way out but back in the direction of her pursuers.

"I hear her going this way," shouted Red. "Come on."

Betty kicked off her shoes to be quieter and continued up the hall. She slipped into an empty room and into a closet.

One of the men produced a flash light. They commenced searching every room. When they got to Betty's room they looked under the bed and in the bathroom. Betty slipped out behind them back into the hall, but they caught her before she could run twenty feet.

"You don't need all those clothes for this," said Red. "Here, I'll help you get 'em off."

While one of the men held her, Red took out his pocket knife and cut away her shirt and pants leaving a bleeding gash where he cut her skin in the process. She struggled free, but was grabbed and held more firmly as Red finished cutting away her panties and bra.

"Shine the light on this little runner," said Red. "Let's see what she looks like."

Stripped of her clothes, stripped of her dignity, she stood quivering in fear and humiliation with tears running down her cheeks.

"Not too shabby as bossy bitches go. On a scale of one to ten, I would give her maybe a four," said Red. "Who wants to be first?"

She was forced to the cold hard floor and one by one they had their way with her.

How can this be happening to me? thought Betty. Lord, you have always protected me. Where have you gone? Why have you abandoned me? She struggled to get free, but it was useless. Then the thought came to her, this must be some kind of a test. What kind of test? She thought of the brutality of these men. She thought of the humiliation, the violation of her sanctity. It was unwarranted, unforgivable. Her inclination was to hate these brutes. That is it, I must forgive them. I must love them…OH, heavens can I really love them?

Red was last. He took pleasure in being especially rough with her. His foul breath repelled her. His whiskers scratched her face as he bit her neck hard while thrusting himself into her. It gave him pleasure to inflict pain while violating her.

All the while, Betty was telling him, "I forgive you. You are a child of God. I can see the holiness in you. You don't understand what you are doing."

At last she felt him exploding into her.

"Anyone want any more of this?" he asked.

They all declined and Betty felt somewhat relieved. Now it was over. They would go away and let her try to put herself back together. It was not to be. Red put his hands around her neck and choked her to death. If this was some sort of a test for Betty, it was her final exam. There is a special place in heaven for the likes of Nurse Betty Andrews.

While her naked, battered body was abandoned on the cold polished floor of the hospital ward, her soul rose to that joyous reunion of loved ones lost. She was enfolded in love and bliss. Her work was finished.

There is a special place in hell for the likes of Red, but his time was not yet.

Patients remaining in the hospital would die one by one lying in their own filth and starving.

Returning outside, Hammer was impatient. "Where have you guys been? Did you find any narcotics?"

"No."

"Then what took you so long?"

"We took a short break for recreation. Let's get out of here."

Hammer smiled. He had gotten the diesel. It was a good night.

CHAPTER SIX

The Larsons and the Harveys were insulated from the turmoil brewing all over the nation and around the world. While they were sawing down bee trees and collecting acorns, unemployment in towns and cities continued to rise. Desperate men and women roamed the county looking for work. Astronauts stranded on the International space station were wondering if what was left of NASA and their Russian counterparts would be able to put together a rescue mission to bring them home.

Members of the armed forces were not being paid. From around the world, from Korea, from Germany, from Afghanistan, and Iraq, they struggled to find their own way home, because the government (what government?) could not arrange for their transportation. One large contingent pirated a cargo ship at gunpoint to sail them back to the once great United States of America. They returned only to find no work. The unemployment numbers rose even more by their arrival but who was counting?

The dollar was deemed worthless in countries around the world. In America, people tried to us dollars because there was no alternative other than a few gold and silver coins. Barter became the order of the day. Food was the most valued medium of exchange.

News of exactly what was going on in the world was spotty. The Harveys listened to WBAP Radio on the car radio for a few days, but soon it was no longer able to broadcast. Some news came from Larson's ham radio.

People lost all confidence in their corrupt government and corporations who helped corrupt them. There was no authority left but force of arms. Some smaller communities pulled themselves together better than the larger cities and towns, in forming armed militias to protect themselves. They pooled resources. Farmers could bring their produce in and trade at farmer's markets. It was now early October. The growing season was over and winter was approaching.

One morning, Larson came up with an Idea of how they might get gas for Fred's car. He put two five gallon gas cans in the bed of the pickup, hooked up the trailer mounted arc welder to the back, and asked Fred to go to town with him. "I don't know why I didn't think of this sooner. The arc welder has a generator. If we can find a gas station with gas in the ground, we can provide the electricity to pump it."

"Should we take our guns?" asked Fred.

"You better. I brought mine," said Larson.

The highway was deserted. Once in town, hardly anything was moving. Dick pulled into the first service station/ convenience store and the two went in. The shelves were bare. An attendant looking like he just got off the boat from India sat behind the counter pointing a shot gun at them.

"Do you have gasoline for sale?" asked Fred.

"We have a little premium left. The regular is gone. But we can't pump it. The electricity is out, you know."

Larson continued inside and shut the door behind him. "Point that gun someplace else. You are making me nervous," he said. "We have a generator. We can provide the electricity."

"Premium goes for thirty dollars a gallon" said the attendant. "Of course you can wait a week and the price will probably be thirty five dollars a gallon if we have any left."

"Is there any food for sale in town?" asked Larson.

"Not that I've heard of."

"I don't suppose any other service stations would have any regular gas, would they?" asked Fred.

"Not likely. And I wouldn't leave my truck unattended out there. People are stealing gas out of all the unattended vehicles. They don't siphon. Instead, they just poke a hole in the bottom of the gas tanks."

Fred didn't know what to do. Filling the two gas cans in Larson's truck would cost three hundred dollars. That was most of the cash he had left in the world. Still, all along, he had said if Larson would help him find gas, he would move on down the road. But where would they go? Everywhere would be the same and he would be broke and without a job. Still, he had promised he would buy gas and move on. "I'll take ten gallons worth." He said. He went to the pickup to fill the cans while Larson worked out a way to get electricity to the pump.

Back at El Rancho, they stopped at the stable and put the gas in Fred's car. Then Larson invited him to the house for coffee. Helen would be there helping with whatever Joyce needed.

When they arrived, the ladies were sitting at the table chatting. Josh was out in the woods foraging for food.

Fred related their experience in town while Joyce brewed a fresh pot of coffee. "Anyway," he finished. "We have gas now. I guess we can drive on down to the coast like we originally planned."

"Oh, please don't leave," said Joyce from the kitchen. I don't know what we would do without you."

"She's right," said Larson. "I figured you would be a burden, but you turned out to be a blessing for us. You won't find anything better wherever you go."

Helen remembered their ordeal leaving Dallas. Would it be any better on the coast if they could make it that far? "Fred, if they will have us, I think we will be better off staying here."

"I'm getting damn tired of this diet of fish, honey, and acorns," said Fred, "but at least we are eating. Maybe you're right."

Larson cleared his throat. He was about to deliver one of his speeches. "We can help you with food. Throughout history there have been wars, famines, floods, hurricanes, and other disasters. People insure their cars, their lives, their houses. Joyce and I insured our food supply. After an ice storm and a tornado, we decided to take stocking up on food seriously. We were influenced by our Mormon friends who said they were encouraged by their church to always keep a two year supply of food on hand. We went with them to a canning facility near Dallas run by their church. We canned peaches and chili. "

"So you stocked up on Peaches and chili?" asked Helen,

"No. On all kinds of food. People have been buying guns and stocking up on ammunition recently anticipating civil unrest or a breakdown in services. They might have better considered having some food on hand and let the crazies shoot it out while saner folks stay inside.

"For a while we kept our food in twelve chests. There was enough food in each chest to last us a month. We labeled each chest with a different month, January, February, etc. After a year, any food we hadn't used out of the chest, we donated to the local food pantry for the poor. In time the system became hard to keep up with. We switched to freeze - dried long term storage by a company called SamAndy. For about a thousand dollars they sold a year's supply of freeze-dried food for two in cans all conveniently boxed up. The same package recently, a dozen or so years later goes for around three thousand dollars. Kept in a temperature controlled environment, freeze dried food should remain good for up to twenty-five years. Our thousand dollar purchase of food is the cheapest insurance we ever bought."

Larson looked accusingly at Fred. "I'll bet even with all the signs pointing to an economic and social breakdown you didn't think to put aside any food."

Fred looked sheepish. "I did buy a couple of boxes of ammo and put together the emergency evacuation chest FEMA recommends. But no, I guess I should have put aside some canned goods. I didn't think things could get so bad."

"We haven't told you about our food stash until now," said Larson. "We haven't shared this with anyone else. Rather than keeping all our savings in worthless paper money, we converted some of it into food to keep on hand as life insurance. On the other hand, what kind of friend would we be if we are unwilling to share when times get hard? Now with banks, the stock market, and dollar in trouble, a food storage plan makes even more sense. But for most people it is too late."

Joyce poured another round of coffee. "Recently Dick suggested to friends and relatives they should stock up on food" she said. "They put aside a few canned goods and figured that would do. I pointed out that it would only last a month. Why don't you get some fifty pound sacks of beans and rice? It may be pretty boring eating, but will sustain you in a famine and you get a lot more bang for your dollar than canned goods."

Larson sipped his coffee. "We stored additional dry food items in five foot long, four inch PVC pipe capped off at both ends," he added. "Mostly it is rice, but there is also salt, sugar, flour, honey, beans, popcorn, and other stuff we figure will keep. On each cylinder we write the contents and date. Recently I got to wondering how well the rice was doing, so I opened a container that had been sealed for thirteen years. Kept dry and cool, the rice was still good.

"More important, we have good water. You can live three weeks without food, but only three days without water. Even when there is no electricity to get water out of our well, you notice, we have water. From the beginning when we moved to the country we wanted to be self-sufficient. The power outage from the ice storm made us wary of depending on electricity from the power company. We put in a cistern.

You can make most any water safe to drink by bringing it to a rolling boil for ten minutes. At first we3 kept chlorine bleach on hand to treat our water, but later learned bleach degrades 20% a year until it is nothing but salt and water. Now we keep Sodium Hypochlorite on hand in powdered form. It keeps. It is the stuff they use to treat swimming pools. A heaping teaspoon of 78% to two gallons of water makes a good stock solution. Add one part stock to 100 parts of water to purify it. The stock solution will degrade too. We only mix enough for a few weeks at a time.

"I built a forty by forty foot shop next to the well. The roof has an area of 1936 square feet. Every inch of rainfall collects twelve hundred gallons of water for the cistern. In the shop I put in a room containing two 1,500 gallon tanks. Every time it rains, fresh rainwater flushes out the tanks. Since the shop is up on a hill above the house, the cistern gravity-feeds water to the house when we lose electricity."

"I notice there isn't much water pressure at the stable, just a trickle," said Helen.

"But at least you have water, said Larson. "Not all my water projects work out like I plan. Years ago while I still lived in Dallas, we had some acreage outside of Fairfield. We kept a camping trailer, a shed to keep the motorcycles in, and a shallow well and septic tank. The kids and I would go down on weekends to ride motorcycles and get away from the city.

"One weekend we went down and found thieves had broken into the shed and stolen motorcycles and even the well pump that was just sitting by the well on the ground.

"The well had Thirty six inch casings. I bought a new pump and pressure tank and suspended them inside the casings. Took off the top section and put the lid back on. Then I covered it over with dirt. No one would know where the well was. They couldn't steal the pump again. Sometimes I am so smart I surprise myself. Months later when there was a malfunction in the water supply I couldn't find the well. DARN!

"We can supplement your rations assured Dick. "Suppose you have dinner with us each evening. That freeze dried food won't last a year for the five of us including Josh, but it will get us through the winter till we can plant a spring garden. Besides, we have the chickens to give us eggs and fish from the lake. We won't starve, but you might if you leave here."

Fred didn't want to leave anyway. He felt he had to suggest it since that was the original agreement for letting them stay. "Okay, if you will have us. We are sure beholden to you for being so generous."

CHAPTER SEVEN

One Sunday morning after living on El Rancho for a month, Fred suggested he, Helen, and Josh go to church.

"What for?" asked Helen. "We've never been church goers. Besides, I don't have a thing to wear. I just gathered up a few old clothes when we left home, nothing to wear to church. We go in dressed like this, and people will think we are just homeless people."

Fred sighed. "That is what we are, Helen. Besides, this is a Christian nation, or it was till recently. It is high time Josh gets exposed to his spiritual side. He probably thinks he is just a guy trying to make it in this world rather than an eternal spiritual being having a brief experience in the physical realm."

Reluctant, Helen groped for excuses. "Where is the church? I haven't seen one close by."

"There is a Methodist church two miles up the road. We haven't met our neighbors. All the social life out here in the country revolves around the church. These folks don't congregate in bars. In fact they vote dry whenever the vote comes up. If we want to expand our circle of friends, we better go to church."

Josh could see no use in going to church. He had set his traps to catch critters. A nice squirrel, rabbit, coon or armadillo was always a welcome addition to their diet. Possum was a bit greasy and stringy, but still… He was tired of fish all the time. Larson had coached him in several tricks in trapping. He even taught the boy to make a crossbow and where best to ambush a deer. All the same his dad was insistent. They bathed using a bucket once a week. This morning they added an extra bath for the week. Josh put on his best jeans and wiped off his shoes.

They set off on foot. No need to waste gas for two miles in the car.

The church was a one story, one room affair with white aluminum siding.

Arriving a few minutes before the service started, they were the objects of great curiosity. Not many strangers came to services, particularly lately. The congregation was polite and asked who they were and where they came from.

When the service started, Josh found it about as exciting as washing dishes and wondered why they walked so far for this.

A deacon went to the pulpit and led the first hymn. Then he recognized Brother Bob who had raised his hand.

Brother Bob rose, but did not move to the front of the congregation. He just stood at his pew. "I want to ask all of you to pray for Sister Melba. Also please welcome Mr. and Mrs. Harvey and their son, Josh. The Harveys are refugees from the chaos in Dallas and are staying as guests of Dick and Joyce Larson."

Everyone turned and gawked at them. Josh hated to be stared at that way. It wasn't all bad though. The prettiest girl he had ever seen was staring at him. She was wearing a blue dress, had blonde hair, and was about his age with dimples that creased her cheeks as she smiled at him. He turned red with embarrassment. He hadn't had a lot of exposure with girls and was just beginning to notice how interesting they were. Interesting, maybe, but scary. The girl staring at him that way made him feel inadequate, like maybe he couldn't pass inspection on close scrutiny.

The deacon led two more hymns.

This was not the Sunday for the traveling circuit preacher to be there. He probably wouldn't be back anyway with the shortage of gas. He was a senior year seminary student. In his absence, the congregation broke up into small groups for Bible study.

When the service was over, folks stood around outside and visited. The pretty girl walked over to Josh. "Hi, I'm Ginger. Glad to meet you Josh."

Josh instinctively backed up when she got in his space. There was a curb behind him. He tripped over it and fell backward into a rose bush. His face turned red again as he got up bleeding from the thorns. He could think of nothing to say.

Ginger smiled her dimpled smile. "You're lucky, Josh. You can date all the girls around here. I'm related to most of the boys. Hope to see you around, Josh." She turned and went back to be with her parents.

Back at El Rancho, Fred related their experience at church to Joyce and Larson.

"It is good that you went, said Dick. You need to know the neighbors, but you may always be an outsider. We have been living here for thirty years, but are still 'not from around here.' Country East Texans are an odd lot, inbred and clannish. They will tack a sign on their fence saying 'WHERE JESUS IS LORD,' then sell you a sick cow they know will soon die. Still in all, when the tornado scattered everything we owned all over the county, those same people tripped all over themselves offering help." Larson's expression darkened. "The way things are going, we must band with these people for our mutual protection. We need them and they need us."

Larson was right about his neighbors. The Harveys went to church every Sunday. They were careful not to say how things were done in the city. Folks were polite. They brought clothes for them and bedding when they learned they lived in a stable. Yet, the Harveys were considered almost aliens from another planet called Dallas. On the up side for Josh, Ginger was there every Sunday. Josh took to going to the Wednesday evening services as well though Fred and Helen declined. They were surprised at how interested Josh was in saving his soul. Ginger attended the Wednesday evening services as well.

CHAPTER EIGHT

Roving bands of desperate people were spreading out from the cities looking for food in the country. Larson's El Rancho sat in cattle country. The land was poor and best suited for growing hay. There were few fields to be gleaned for food, but a slaughtered cow feeds a number of people. An isolated rancher could scarcely defend his few livestock against a hungry mob. Some marauders had acquired horses and developed tactics to come at night and raid farmhouses from all sides at once. Life had little value for these raiders save their own lives. Cars and trucks had been abandoned for lack of fuel. Not all the gangs had horses. Small armies roamed the land on foot.

A one lane county road ran in front of El Racho. Larson called a meeting of everyone living on the road to see what could be done for mutual protection. A strategy emerged, blocking off a three mile section of the road. They dug a ditch six feet deep across the road at each end and erected a chain link fence outside of the trench. Obscure passes through high barricades on adjacent properties at each end could gain access to the road. A mob would hopefully take the path of least resistance and pass them by. Guards were posted on horseback to keep watch twenty four hours a day over the access to the protected stretch. Should looters attempt to trespass, the guard would ride off to alert all the residents. Strategies were devised and practiced to repel invaders. A guard duty schedule was posted at the church.

Josh was devastated when he was dropped from consideration for guard position because he had never ridden a horse.

` Ginger rode horses. She volunteered to teach him and would let him use one of her horses. Leading a second horse for Josh, she daily rode to El Rancho. With no school in session, Ginger had all the time in the world to teach Josh even if it took weeks or months. She seemed willing to spend years.

Her parents were not fooled. They had noticed the growing bond between Ginger and Josh. It shouldn't take that much time to train Josh. She would leave home in the morning, join Josh for fishing and hunting, and then they would ride off into the countryside for the rest of the day. Ginger's father began making noises that the two young people were getting too serious in their relationship. When Josh was accepted as a mounted guard, her father forbade Ginger from going to El Rancho to "teach" Josh any further. He had become so concerned about his daughter's interest in the new city boy he would only allow them to talk to one another at church where he could keep an eye on them.

The most undesirable stretch of guard duty was the grave yard shift between midnight and six AM. Most complained to the scheduler when assigned to it. Ginger volunteered for it and Josh slipped quietly out of his stall to join her whenever she was assigned to stand watch. They talked the hours away alone in the dark together.

Josh considered Ginger the most perfect creature in all creation. Why she would even bother to speak to him was a mystery. Ginger adored him. The powerful chemistry of youth, hormones, and two souls destined for each other from before they were born wove its magic. Josh did his best to be the wonderful person Ginger thought he was.

CHAPTER NINE

Larson, Fred, and Josh prepared a fall garden. "I've never been an avid gardener," said Larson. "I often put in a few tomato plants because home grown tomatoes taste better than those in the grocery. Some years when it was cool in the spring and the urge hit me, I planted a vegetable garden, but by harvest time, I had abandoned the project. It was too hot and the weeds had taken over.

"Just because I'm not cut out to be a gardener doesn't mean I'm not prepared. Being a survivalist, I was always aware that I could not stock up enough food to last forever in dire times. I built up a sizeable library on gardening, learned procedures from neighbors, and stocked up on seeds"

Josh and his dad hoed weeds while Larson talked.

"Some of the seeds from seed companies are hybrids that do not produce seeds for subsequent years. I was careful to avoid these. In addition, I prepared a large garden plot should I ever decide I needed to plant a vegetable crop. I was careful to add soil amendments to build up a fertile base. Now it is the first of October. No fresh vegetables can be bought. I could see trouble coming so I planted beets, peas and tomatoes in August. In September I put in lettuce and carrots. Now it is October and it is time to plant cabbage.

"We need to put in a lot of potatoes come spring," said Larson. "At one time, potatoes saved Europeans from starvation. Hungry invading armies were unfamiliar with potato plants. Not realizing the potatoes were buried beneath, they would pass them by."

Larson continued leaning on his shovel and talking while Fred and Josh worked. "Over the years," he continued, "Joyce and I played survival games. The Boy Scout motto is 'Be prepared.' We moderns have become too soft. We are ill prepared to cope when the electricity goes out. An ice storm once rendered us without electricity for three days. Our neighbors were without electricity to their all electric house for three weeks. We decided then we would always be ready to get on quite well without the electric power company. What if there was another oil embargo? What if those jackasses in Washington screwed things up so bad there was another great depression? What if the dollar became worthless or the government collapsed altogether under its own corruption like it has? What if some crazy dictator in a far off land dropped the bomb? Would an earth sheltered house protect us from fallout? It turns out our house makes an excellent fallout shelter. I bought a kit to check radiation levels to know when it was safe to come out. What skills would we need? What food and water should we stock up on? Would solar power work for us? We played many of these self-sufficiency games, but never from any deep fear. It was more like going on a camping trip knowing we need only get in the car and drive back home if it got too uncomfortable. When that tornado blew us away it became more than just a game."

Gazing over the fence and across an adjoining pasture, Fred could see a large well-appointed house. The grass was not mowed and weeds were taking over. "Who lives over there?"

"No one," said Larson. I'm told some guy out of Dallas bought it and came down only once or twice a year to shoot his guns. I never met him. I heard him shooting a couple of times. He hired some of the locals to keep the place up, but I see they haven't been doing it since all this trouble came. You would think he would come down here and escape the city. Maybe he tried and didn't make it."

Once the seeds were in the ground, Larson suggested they gather up leaves for mulch. There was no shortage. By now they were everywhere. They went out under the trees and Larson drove the tractor while Fred and Josh raked and scooped them into the front-end-loader. Soon, there was a mountain of leaves rotting by the garden.

Larson shut the tractor down so Fred and Josh could hear him talk. Leaning on a hoe, he said, "We want to cover the bare ground with leaves and keep a large pile to rot for compost. We can't get too much organic material in this sand we have for soil. We will mix leaves, old hay, and manure, kitchen scraps, whatever we can find. If we turn it regularly, it will all rot into the perfect mix for tilling into the soil.

"Folks can work themselves to death doing all the chores on a farm," said Larson. "It is no place to get rich and kids raised on a farm flock to the city to avoid the toil. On the other hand, there is a joy to eating home grown tomatoes. Sitting on our private pier, dipping a hook, watching the wildlife, and enjoying a quiet so profound you can almost hear the grass grow is just about as close to heaven as one can get in this life."

He took a swipe at a weed then went back to leaning on his hoe. "In the last great depression many were living on farms where they could grow their own food and not depend on the government. Folks seemed to be more God fearing, kinder, and gentler back then. They were more ready to help each other. Today, smart people are out of the city. Living in a small town is safer, living on a farm, better yet."

Larson had taught Josh to drive the tractor. When the leaves were spread, he sent Josh back on the tractor to the barn. Stepping down off the tractor, Josh snagged his arm on a nail. It ripped a nasty gash that bled freely. He wrapped a rag around it and walked back to where his father and Larson were standing. "I cut my arm on a nail."

"Let me see," said Larson.

Josh pulled the rag back, revealing a gushing slit in the skin.

"Let's get him down to the house," said Fred. Helen is a nurse. She will know what to do for him."

By the time they got to Helen, the bleeding had stopped. She washed the surrounding area and asked if there was any antiseptic available.

"I've got a gallon of Peroxide," said Larson. He disappeared into the back and came out with a bottle.

While Helen cleaned the wound, Larson launched into a long explanation of the history and uses of Hydrogen Peroxide. "It was invented during world war two to treat wounded soldiers." He continued naming a dozen uses for the stuff which is why he stocked so much of it.

While Helen finished bandaging Josh's arm, Joyce brewed a fresh pot of coffee and brought out a bowl of fruit leathers. "During the season, we get more peaches, plums, apples and pears than we can eat. We used to can the extra, but canning is too much trouble. For a while we used the freezer, but Dick didn't like relying on electricity to keep our food. So we started drying our excess fruits and vegetables in an electric dehydrator. You know Dick; he is always in the survival mode. He wasn't happy using electricity to dry the food either. He found a book on a solar powered dehydrator and how to build and use one."

Larson beamed. He was in his element when the conversation moved to his self-sufficiency innovations. He liked to steer the talk in that direction whenever possible, but now Joyce had done it for him.

"Our EXCALIBAR electric dehydrator worked well while we had electricity, explained Larson. "Being a survivalist, I wondered if I couldn't build a solar food dryer. A number of them have been devised using the idea of a box to keep the bugs out and a glass to let the sun in. Eban Fodor takes the idea to a higher level engineering a solar dehydrator that will work most anywhere crops are raised.

FODOR'S SOLAR FOOD DRYER

He published the design in his book, THE SOLAR FOOD DRYER. Now, with the electricity gone, it will come in handy next growing season.

"The trick is to dry the food as quickly as possible without cooking it. Temperature in Fodor's dryer is controlled by adjusting the size of the exiting air vent. Keeping the temperature between 120 and 150 works best. A good solar dryer can heat the air ten to twenty five degrees Celsius above outside temperature and create air movement to carry off the moisture. Fodor's solar dryer usually takes a couple of days to dry most foods. The exposure to sunlight for this brief time does minimal damage to the nutrients and taste of food.

"Fruits should be dried to the point of being leathery while vegetables should be dried till they are brittle.

"Following Fodor's design, I built my own solar dehydrator at a cost less than the fancy EXCALIBER. Fodor's book in paperback used from Amazon sold for less than ten dollars.

"Dried food is half to one fifteenth as bulky as fresh. I store dehydrated food in an air tight container in a cool dark place. They will last a year or longer. This is as long as frozen foods are good. And drying needs no electricity. Fodor's book explains the whole process."

Helen took another bite of fruit leather. "This is really good," she said. "do the neighbors know about all this? If things aren't any better come summer, you need to give classes."

"I got into solar cooking too," Larson said. "I went to Google and typed in 'solar cookers; found an array of solar ovens ranging in price from seventy to four hundred fifty dollars. I bought the Sun Oven. Joyce cooked rabbit stew in it today.

"We are at the mercy of the weather with a solar oven. Early on the temperature in the oven registered two hundred ninety degrees. Later a thin layer of high cirrus clouds came in and the temperature dropped to one hundred fifty degrees. Still, it got the job done and we didn't have to use any propane in the stove. Many in poorer countries around the world have no fuel to cook with.

"Mike and Martha Port in Minneapolis have founded the SOLAR OVEN SOCIETY. For the past several years they have been involved in perfecting their latest model the sport solar oven using recycled soda bottles. The Ports market their cookers in the United States and use the profit to donate shipments to poorer countries around the world. The Sport retailed for one hundred thirty five dollars plus thirty three dollars for shipping. The entire unit weighs only ten pounds. Whereas my little solar oven only has a one foot square chamber, the Sport can accommodate two three point four quart pots. If I had it all to do over again, I believe I would buy the Post's Sport model.

"Time was, when Joyce wanted to make a stew, she put the ingredients in a Crock pot and let it simmer all day. Now, without electricity, we converted our ice chest into a hay box by insulating all around the pot. Joyce heats the pot of stew to boiling on the stove then puts it in the hay box. The residual heat in the pot and contents will continue to cook the stew. After several hours the stew is ready to eat with no electricity needed. Come to think of it, we could have brought it to a boil in the solar cooker and transferred it into the hay box if it clouded over."

CHAPTER TEN

On a cold rainy night in December, Ginger stood guard duty doing the graveyard shift. Josh had come to be with her. A crude guard shack had been erected to afford shelter from rain and wind. Ginger shivered uncontrollably. Josh had brought along a bed roll and the two wrapped themselves in it and held each other tight.

"I'm so hungry, Josh," said Ginger. "We are out of food. The only thing we have had to eat in the past week is the fish and game you brought. I don't think we will survive the winter."

Josh was no longer the self-centered, dull witted, fat kid who had left Dallas in September. Now, trimming down and alert, he was evolving into an accomplished hunter and fisherman who could sit a horse with the best of them. "You won't starve, Ginger. I will see to that." He held her tight and wondered if his words were merely empty promises. What more could he do?

Back at El Rancho, Josh confided his concern for Ginger and her family to the Larsons. Food on El Rancho was adequate though not lavish but the Larsons were unprepared to feed everyone up and down the road lest they ended up starving with everyone else.

KUDZU

"Go to the barn and fetch a couple of shovels and an axe, Josh," said Larson. When Josh returned, they got in the truck and drove toward town. "There is a kudzu patch up the road here," Larson explained. "I asked the owner if I could dig up some of the roots. He begged me to dig them all up."

When they got to the kudzu it was a large area of vines draped over a stand of trees alongside the road. The trees were all dead since the vines had choked off the sunlight to them.

"Kudzu was brought over from Japan years ago," said Larson. "It was thought to be a wonderful plant. The young leaves taste good in salads or cooked like spinach. It makes good cattle fodder. Being a legume, it puts nitrogen into the soil wherever it grows. The government planted it on embankments to control erosion and encouraged farmers to plant it. Like most things the government does, it turned out to be a bad idea. Kudzu is too much of a good thing. Once planted, it takes over everything, especially here in the south. You can't get rid of it."

Josh expected the roots to be small and they would have to dig up a lot of them to feed a family. To his surprise, the root of a single kudzu vine was as large as a man. They dug up two.

Larson drove directly to Ginger's house. Mr. Peterson, Ginger's father heard the truck drive up and came out.

"We brought you something to eat," explained Larson. "Josh here tells me you folks are getting a little hungry. Saw this root up into narrow strips and beat the strips into flour. It is kudzu. They tell me it is used in gourmet cooking."

Mr. Peterson took it gratefully but eyed Josh suspiciously. At first he had been friendly to Josh, but as time went by, he decided Josh was getting too close to his daughter. "How did Josh know we were out of food?" he asked.

"Ginger told me," said Josh.

"When was that? We haven't been to church recently."

Josh knew he had slipped up. Mr. Peterson had not suspected he and Ginger were spending hours together at the guard shack.

"I relieved her when she came off the graveyard shift recently," Josh lied.

They drove back to El Rancho, but Josh knew if Mr. Peterson checked the schedule, he would discover Josh never had guard duty following Ginger.

Joyce was waiting for them when they returned. "Dick, we must do something to feed our little community." She said as they came in the door. "We have people doing round the clock guard over an empty store house. Feeding Ginger and her family isn't enough. There are thirty seven families on three-mile-road and most of them starving."

Larson, the survivalist had also stocked up on fuel. He had converted two 250 gallon propane tanks for gasoline storage. In addition he had installed an oversized propane tank and even filled ten fifty five gallon barrels with diesel fuel though it would run his tractor years longer than he would expect to live. He rarely left the farm with his truck, but he was the only one up and down the road with gasoline to do so. When he did venture out, Fred and Josh came along with guns.

Joyce was right. His neighbors were starving and many would not last the winter. Next morning, he hooked up his sixteen foot farm trailer; put two barrels of diesel on it and invited Fred and Josh to take the 50 mile trip to Tyler where the main office of the Brookshire Grocery chain was located. It proved to be a wasted trip. Supply trucks were not running. Brookshires had no food.

Larson carefully calculated how much gas it would take to drive to the producer of animal feed in another town. He decided it was worth the try. The mill was quiet. It appeared no one was there, but then a man appeared from the head office. "I'm afraid you are too late," the man said. The soup kitchen in Dallas came and picked up most everything. The only thing we have left is soybeans and some field corn. We feed that to the livestock, but people aren't interested."

Josh was horrified. He was prepared to move heaven and earth to see to it that Ginger got enough to eat. Where else could they turn?

"We'll take it." said Larson. "What do you want for it?"

The man thought for a minute. "We no longer take dollars. What's your barter?"

"How about a hundred gallons of diesel for a trailer load of soy beans and corn?"

The man shook his head. "It will cost you a lot more than that."

Fred fingered a coin in his pocket. "Would you take a one ounce gold eagle instead?"

The man pondered. He could tell these three were desperate. He could name his price. "I'll take the coin and the diesel."

"Okay," said Larson, "if you will bag it up in fifty pound bags so it is easier to handle."

Driving back to El Rancho with a trailer full of corn and soy beans, Fred asked, "What are we going to do with all those beans? I never heard of people eating soy beans."

"Sure you have," said Larson. "You've heard of tofu haven't you? In Japan where there is high population density people rely on soy beans for their protein. Here in the states we are spoiled to beef, pork and chicken. The United States is the largest producer of soy beans in the world. We feed them to our animals. Now that famine stalks the land, we must adapt to the new reality and move lower on the food chain. Soy is where we need to be, actually soy and corn. You need a grain to go with the soy to make a complete protein."

Josh was quicker to pick up on new ideas than his father. "We have enough here to save the neighborhood from starvation all winter, I'll bet," he said.

CHAPTER ELEVEN

Reluctant to store the soy beans in the barn where rodents could get to them, Larson took them to the house. All the furniture was removed from a guest bedroom and bags of corn and beans were stacked floor to ceiling. A search through Larson's survival library yielded THE BOOK OF TOFU by William Shurtleff and Akiko Aoyagi. In the following days a flurry of activity turned the Larson house into a tofu factory.

Joyce and Helen went up and down the road distributing samples and inviting all the women of the households to come to the Larson's on Saturday to form a co-operative for feeding the hungry which turned out to be everyone. At the meeting, the ladies voted to meet every Saturday at the church to study the uses of wild plants for nutrition and healing. Since clothes could no longer be purchased in town, an apparel swap was instituted where each family brought in outgrown clothes for use by anyone who needed them.

Some of the elderly suffered extreme chills in their homes when the propane ran out. As the ladies got organized, they pressed all able bodied men into sawing and splitting wood for fire places and wood burning stoves. Homemade wood stoves were improvised from barrels where needed.

Before the fall of the dollar the neighborhood was a collection of strangers. The church had brought some together, but many were left out. Now the church was the common meeting place for all. It was not only a place of worship, but a community center where all met to share for the common good. In times past, the opulence enjoyed by these rural East Texans had kept neighbors apart. Now they banned together for survival.

Larson marveled when he met a man who lived directly across the road from him for eight years yet he had never seen him.

The elderly were particularly valued. Their experience and wisdom was treasured. They had survived the first great depression and brought with them memories and skills of how things were done in a simpler time before antibiotics, television, the internet, fast food and so much more. One afternoon, Mary Lowery told of her recollections of the depression.

One afternoon Mary Lowery told of her recollections of the Great Depression. "I was born in 1922 and remember the depression years well. I didn't know there was anything else for us until the 1940's when world war two brought it to an end.

"We lived on sandy land of around 300 acres owned by Papa and The Land Bank. There were three boys and three girls. We walked about three miles to school until I was in fourth grade. We all had our chores. The girls and Mama never plowed in the fields but we gathered and we always had a spring and fall garden. We were never hungry. We canned and dried food during harvest to carry us through the winter and Papa always had cows and pigs. We had plenty of butter and milk. When we didn't have crops to gather or garden stuff to can and preserve we picked berries for the neighbors in season to make a little spending money. We drew our water from a well and the outhouse was some distance from the house. Papa built a trough a foot high and a foot wide by about 6 feet long and tarred it so it would be waterproof. There was a little trough running from the well to a screened in back porch to the 6 foot trough to pour water in. This is where we cooled the milk

"Papa really never was a farmer. He farmed but he was by nature a trader. He peddled watermelons and other crop stuff we didn't need for our use and he butchered beef and peddled it. He sold milk and cream in big cans and later sold bottled milk. Mama would mold butter into a pound-size and he would sell that.

"Mama made all our clothes. The girl's clothes were made over from hand-me- down clothes relatives had given us. We were as well

dressed as any one because Mama was an expert seamstress.
I well remember the W.P.A. and the C.C.C. camp and the rock fence the C.C.C. built around our school yard and the other projects they did. Those in Washington were crazy. I also remember the slaughtered and thrown away beef, and the plowed under crops, that is crops that were just plowed into the ground rather than harvesting for food. I remember the handouts some people got who wouldn't work and Papa receiving "pea checks" for the plowed under pea crop. We debated both sides of those issues in high school debate teams.

Yes, I remember the depression Years."

Loretta Smith told what she remembered of those days.

"I remember the great depression. Dad was a watch repairman in Arkansas until the 1930's when no one had any money to get their watches and clocks fixed. Dad took his inheritance and bought a thirty eight acre farm with a two bedroom house on it in Miller County Arkansas. There were seven of us kids, all girls except Kevin the youngest.

"Unlike many, we never went hungry. We were a Christian family. We didn't work on Sunday, but we worked hard the rest of the time. There was love in the family so it didn't seem like such hard work.

"We lived three miles from the nearest town but hobos would show up asking to work for a bite to eat. Someone in town must have been telling them they could find food if they walked out there. Mother never turned anyone away. She would find a chore for them to do while she fixed something.

"We raised our own food. There was no money to buy any. We had cows, pigs, and chickens. There was a mule to pull the plow and a wagon. There was little meat. Mostly we had cornbread, potatoes, peas, and greens. We also grew lettuce, carrots, squash, onions, cabbage, beets and turnips. I remember an apple and a peach tree, hickory nuts, and berries to pick in season. We canned the fruit, but couldn't can the vegetables. You would need a pressure cooker and it was impossible to keep the heat up on the old wood stove to properly do the vegetables. In the fall when it got cold enough, we would slaughter two big hogs and cure them in the smoke house.

'The outhouse was far away from the house down wind to keep the smell away. We drew water from the well with a bucket. Electricity hadn't reached that far out yet. We did have a battery powered radio with an antenna strung along the fence. Now, here we are again with no electricity.

'We made our own lye-soap out of old grease, cracklings, and bits of fat and gristle from the hogs. This was mixed with lye leached out of wood ashes. Baths were often sponge baths out of a dishpan. Soda was used for toothpaste.

"There was a small shallow pond on the place, home for snakes. We didn't go there. I never learned to swim.

"Of the seven kids, five of us went to college. We worked our way through. I went for a teaching degree. I earned my room and board working in the cafeteria and paid the tuition with other odd jobs. I did a lot of babysitting. I would often get home about midnight and have to be at the cafeteria at five in the morning.

"We made dresses out of feed sacks. If someone got sick, we prayed, used remedies Mother knew from her childhood, or consulted neighbors for cures. We were well fed and generally healthy.

"Self-respect and pride in cleanliness and in keeping our word were emphasized. We were taught to see beauty, beauty in nature and in our love. Neighbor kids would come and delight in staying for dinner (lunch) because we had plenty of food and maybe even a berry cobbler. We had swings hanging from a couple of trees and a jump rope from an old rope, no longer useable with the livestock; Things to play with were homemade. We made houses by drawing lines in the dirt under a shade tree with doors and windows marked and a piece of a limb to sit on. Dishes were used jar lids adorned with mud pies and cakes. Our imaginations were encouraged. We blossomed on praise and encouragement."

Home medical remedies were especially useful. One man bragged about his silver colloidal generator.

"When I woke up this morning I could feel the onset of flu symptoms," reported George Sanders. There was the sore throat, pressure in my sinuses and a bit of a headache. I have owned a colloidal silver generator for years. I generated some for virtually no cost and inhaled it using a nebulizer bought at the drug store. I plugged it into Larson's solar generator. The symptoms went away. Some studies say colloidal silver is good against acne, aides, allergies, arthritis, athlete's foot, boils, burns, diabetes, and a bunch of other things. One testimonial claimed a cure for pneumonia. Others say it has no proven value for anything. My wife asked her registered nurse niece what she does for a cold. She said colloidal silver. Colloidal silver was in common use before the nineteen forties when antibiotics came in.

"Before the electricity went out, I found colloidal silver for sale on the internet at $25 for an eight and a half ounce bottle. With my battery powered generator, I made 16 ounces for the cost of a little distilled water and the nine volt battery that has been in the generator for years. I don't remember what I paid for my generator back then, but I find them for sale on the net for $130 up to $400. That seems a lot considering my generator is essentially two wires with clamps on them attached to a nine volt battery and two silver electrodes (coat hanger thick pure silver wires eight inches long.) The silver electrodes are placed in sixteen ounces of distilled water with a pinch of salt added. The wires from the battery are clamped one to each electrode. A bluish cloud of colloidal silver is emitted. It takes eleven minutes to generate the desired strength of solution."

Nell Johnson talked about prescription drugs and how hard it was to stock up because the druggist would only give what the Doctor ordered. "I could see this crash coming," she said. "I talked my doctor into prescribing more than I really needed so I could save up for hard times."

A group got together and wrote down home remedies that were in common use in the distant past. Helen was the one nurse in the community. There were no doctors. She was kept busy tending to local health problems. Much of her training was centered on modern pharmaceuticals that were no longer available. Her education went into fast mode learning of the old ways, trying them out and determining which worked and which did not.

Helen and Fred were invited to stay with Nell Johnson who had a spare bedroom. It was a welcome relief from sleeping in the unheated stable. Helen spent her mornings visiting with Joyce when she wasn't involved with nursing duties. Fred continued to help Larson. They knew they owed plenty to the Larsons who took them in and probably saved their lives. Thankfully, Josh, Helen, and Fred were still welcome at the Larsons' table for supper. Dick and Joyce offered a more varied diet than the rest of the community enjoyed.

Brother Mike, an elderly preacher came out of retirement to minister to them. He was not a Methodist, so the congregation voted to make the church non-denominational.

One morning Frank Peters was drinking coffee at the church center when his speech began slurring just before he collapsed. His face went slack on one side - - classic symptoms of a stroke. Friends rushed him to Helen who did what she could; she kept mum about feeling powerless to help Mr. Peters. She made him comfortable on a cot in the Larson's living room.

When Brother Mike arrived at the church they told him about Frank. Brother Mike dropped to his knees and prayed fervently for him. He asked others to do the same.

Two hours later Frank walked back into the church apparently healed. Helen could only attribute it to a temporary spike in blood pressure. No one believed her. Brother Mike was held as a bit of a saint and folks took a new interest in their prayer life.

Years before, soon after moving into the neighborhood, Dick Larson decided he had little in common with the locals. He quit trying to have much to do with them. Now with the tofu project underway, he was in constant contact with them. He found they had practical knowledge he needed. Most had grown up on a farm, pulling calves, castrating hogs, and milking cows. They knew what crops would grow and when to plant them. His new friends were familiar with the newest fertilizer, herbicides, and pesticides, but also had memories of what was used in past eras before chemicals were available.

CHAPTER TWELVE

Josh received spotty reports of conditions in Dallas. He mourned the sure death of his former friends. He still slept in the stable, but considered himself lucky.

Across the fields, he could see the big house of the rich owner from Dallas who once visited occasionally. It intrigued him. The man may have been rich, but apparently not too bright. Why hadn't he made his escape to the country while he could? He must be dead by now or he would be here.

One morning Josh walked over to check out the place. Weeds grew everywhere. He tried the doors but they were locked. An upstairs window was open a couple of inches. Using a ladder from the barn he climbed up to gain entrance through the window. He felt uneasy breaking and entering, but who would know or care? Inside the house all was in order, waiting the return of the owner who would probably never come. The bed in the master bedroom looked inviting. There were extra blankets in the closet. What difference if he slept in it instead of on the hay in that drafty stable of the Larsons? Down stairs a cozy fireplace called his name. He envisioned sitting before a warming fire on cold nights. What could it hurt? If the owner came back, Josh could simply leave. He would steal nothing. Why would anyone care? Who could argue with his reasoning? He moved in. The Larsons and his parents put up scant protest when he told them. They could understand his desire to find better lodging. The world was different now. Survival was the game. Josh would be a survivor.

Sitting before the fire in the evenings alone in his new house, Josh dreamed of the day when he and Ginger would live together and raise a family. The thought of it warmed his spirits more than the fire itself.

On a bitter cold night in January, Ginger again had the security watch from midnight to six. Josh went over to keep her company. They wrapped themselves in his bedroll and talked.

About two o'clock, Ginger's father came in shining a light in their eyes. "You son of a bitch!" he said. "I told you to stay away from my daughter!"

Brandishing a pistol, he aimed at Josh's head. "No!" shouted Ginger and pushed his arm spoiling his aim as the shot went off and the bullet flew by Josh's ear. He bolted from the shed and ran into the night. Mr. Peterson gave chase, but lost Josh in the woods. Josh had never been so scared.

Early next morning, Josh went to the Larson's. His parents were there. He related what happened.

"Josh, you better leave Ginger alone. Forget her," said Helen. "Mr. Peterson has a right to protect his daughter."

The thought of such a thing was not something Josh was ready to consider. He loved Ginger more than life itself.

While they were discussing Josh's plight, there was a knock at the door. It was Ginger looking for Josh. Her eyes filled with tears. She hadn't slept. "Dad threw me out of the house. He called me all kinds of ugly names like whore and slut. I don't know where to turn, what to do."

"You aren't pregnant, are you?" asked Fred.

"No, I'm a virgin. Josh and I haven't been together in that way. We were just talking."

"Is that right, Josh?" asked Joyce.

"Yes ma'am, but I want to marry Ginger."

"You are too young." There is plenty of time for that later on," said Fred.

"Why are we too young?" asked Josh. "Dad, I have been taking better care of her than Mr. Peterson. I have brought her food when Mr. Peterson could not. I have a house for us to live in and her father has kicked her out of his. Times are different now. It is not like it was. We don't need a college education to get ahead in this new world order. Ginger and I already have the skills necessary."

"He may have a point there," said Larson. "I remember my father telling of when he was born that life expectancy was only forty-something. This new reality is more like it was back then. People shouldn't wait till they are twenty-five or thirty to have children. They may not live long enough to raise their kids."

"I think it is against the law in this state for kids your age to marry," said Helen.

"What law? What state? There aren't any laws any more as far as I can see," Josh countered.

Fred turned to Ginger. "Do you want to marry Josh, Ginger? Have you two been talking about that?"

"No we haven't exactly discussed it; I would like it very much."

Brother Mike was summoned. When asked if he would perform a wedding ceremony, he said he would have to see a marriage license.

"There are no licenses being issued any more as far as we know," said Fred.

Brother Mike pondered the problem. "This is unusual. Let's go to the church. The congregation is the law of our community now. It is the only law we have. If there are no valid reasons why I shouldn't, I will perform the ceremony. Ginger's parents must have a say in this though."

At church, there were people milling around waiting to eat. Brother Mike told them Josh and Ginger wanted to get married and he would perform the ceremony if there were no objections. Billy Bob was sent to the Peterson's to ask them to come and offer their say. Billy Bob returned saying Mr. Peterson refused and his wife appeared afraid to come without him.

Brother Mike looked at his watch. It was ten o'clock. He turned to Josh and Ginger. "Are you two ready to get married today?"

Josh held Ginger's hand and looked into her pretty face. "I am, if you are."

Ginger squeezed his hand and returned his gaze. "Oh, yes!"

"The wedding will be at two." Brother Mike announced.

There was a flurry of activity. Josh was hurriedly dressed for the wedding. A white shirt and a suit that almost fit came from the clothes swap. He was supplied with a pair of shiny shoes. He had worn only boots since he found some that fit from the clothes swap weeks before.

Joyce Larson dug into a closet and came out with her wedding dress. With few alterations, it fit Ginger perfectly. Then she and Helen baked a wedding cake.

At five minutes of two, everyone from up and down the road sat in their pews when Mr. and Mrs. Peterson came in and took their usual seats. Ginger went to her father. "Daddy, will you walk down the aisle with me?"

"I will not," he said not looking at her but staring sternly straight ahead.

Brother Mike began the ceremony with, "Dearly beloved."

He got to the part where he said, “If anyone here can show cause why this man and this woman should not be joined in Holy Matrimony, let him speak now or forever after hold his peace.” Ginger’s father cleared his throat. ”Ahem.”

The entire community was aware of the story of Charlie Peterson trying to shoot Josh and then kicking Ginger out of his house. Would he try to break up the ceremony?

His wife kicked his foot. All eyes turned to the pair. A long silence followed.

The ceremony continued, finishing with Brother Mike saying, “I now pronounce you man and wife.”

As a wedding present, a neighbor supplied them with a setting hen on a dozen fertile eggs. Another neighbor donated a milk goat with two kids.

CHAPTER THIRTEEN

Ginger continued standing the graveyard shift at one end of three-mile road. Josh kept her company. One night the vigil paid off. Hammer and his gang showed up at the barrier on a cattle rustling raid. Most were on horseback. They brought a large cattle truck to haul livestock back to Dallas for slaughter. Josh recognized Hammer's voice from the night his family left home. He barked orders.

"Howard, get the bolt cutters and cut the chain link fence. If there isn't something valuable here, they wouldn't have such security measures set up."

"Red, you take twenty men and make raids on any farm houses you come to. The rest of us will herd cattle."

In the darkness, the gang could not see Josh, Ginger, and the guardhouse nestled in the underbrush inside the fence. The couple could see the rustlers in the headlights of the cattle truck.

Josh whispered to Ginger, "Get on your horse and go alert everyone. Tell them to come quickly, armed and ready to shoot. I have my crossbow. I will slow them down."

Ginger quietly mounted up and left.

Josh armed his crossbow. As the man with the bolt cutters approached the fence, Josh took aim and shot an arrow through the chain-link fence and into his chest. He was dead before he hit the ground.

"What happened to him?" asked Hammer.

The crossbow killed silently.

One of the men went forward to check him out. "He has an arrow in his chest. He is dead."

Josh put an arrow in the man kneeling over his dead comrade. He crumpled and fell mortally wounded on the body of the first.

A number of flashlights came on illuminating the area on Josh's side of the fence. Josh ducked back into the shadows before he was seen.

The rustlers were spooked. Two of their number were dead from arrows shot from out of the darkness. Who knows how many defenders there were.

"Get the truck up here and drive through that fence," ordered Hammer sounding furious. "Someone pull the bodies out of the way."

Not one was willing to come forward and risk another arrow.

"Okay," said Hammer, "Drive the truck over them, they are dead anyway."

The truck started up and lumbered forward driving forcefully into the chain link fence which gave way allowing the truck to continue into the unseen trench on the other side. Its headlights and radiator were crushed. The cab sloped down. The rig was hopelessly stuck.

"Back it out of there! Back it out of there!" Hammer raged, seeing his well thought out raid falling apart, but the truck was going nowhere.

The driver sat in the cab, afraid to get out for fear he would be the next target of the silent killer or killers. No one knew how many archers were shooting arrows.

Hammer stewed in confusion not knowing how to proceed. Should he retreat, get a new truck, raid some other area on another night? The men stood around offering suggestions. Most were ready to call it a night.

Josh knew all the delay was buying time for the citizens of three mile road to come to the defense.

Not ready to give it up, Hammer pondered his next move. It galled him to have someone with a bow and arrow foil his plan causing him to lose a truck as well. He was motivated now more by revenge than any desire to sack the countryside.

"We are not quitting," said Hammer. "We will teach these yokels a lesson. Spray the area with machinegun fire."

Josh, hearing that, threw himself on the ground behind a tree. Bullets flew above his head. His heart was racing. He was terrified, but determined to stall the raiders as long as possible. When the firing stopped, he scampered back to a safer distance.

"Cut the fence and pull it back out of the way," directed Hammer.

Josh crept forward to take another shot at the raiders. He knew he couldn't kill them all, but if he could slow them down, it would buy more time for reinforcements to show up. If that crowd made it across the trench on their horses, they would surely run him down. He let fly with another arrow, but he was not close enough. He only managed to hit a man in the shoulder. Another burst of machinegun fire forced him back.

"Get the ramp from the back of the truck, and put it across the trench so we can ride our horses across," ordered Hammer.

Fred was the first of the locals to arrive on the scene. It was the first time he had driven his Toyota since they arrived in East Texas. Seeing men with flashlights working at the trench, he stopped some distance short and decided to wait till more defenders came to back him up. He shut down the engine and headlights and got out carrying his shotgun.

First across the ramp on his horse was Hammer. In his fury, seeing the dim outline of Fred standing in front of his car, he boldly galloped at him. Fred was not much of a gun person. He raised his piece to fire, but forgot to take off the safety. Before he could solve his problem, Hammer was upon him knocking him to the ground half under the Toyota. The shotgun went flying out of his grasp.

Fred scooted further under the car trying to get away.

Hammer turned on his flashlight to see where he went. Then he noticed the license number on the Toyota, the number he had memorized when the car ran down his brother in Dallas months before.

Trapped, Fred could hardly move beneath the car.

"Well, well, you son of a bitch! I vowed if I ever caught up with you, I would see you died slowly. The gods are smiling on me tonight," sneered Hammer. With his pistol in one hand and the flash light in the other, he pointed his gun between Fred's eyes and let Fred know he need only pull the trigger and he was dead. Then he shifted his aim and shot him in the thigh.

Pain shot through Fred and he jerked.

Enjoying the slow execution of the man who killed his brother, Hammer took his time letting Fred anticipate the next shot. It confused him for a moment when he felt Josh's arrow pierce his back, but only for a moment before he was dead,

Josh grabbed his father's shotgun and pointed it at the approaching second member of the gang. It was Red. "Your friend is dead," Josh said and I will cut you in two if you don't back off."

Red looked up and saw the rest of the Three Mile Road community coming. Some were on horseback silhouetted in the headlights of the few who still had fuel to drive. He turned his horse and rode back across the ramp. The element of surprise was no longer with them. "Come on," he said. "Let's go home.

Josh pulled the trigger to fire a parting shot to hurry Red on his way. But the safety was still on. In the passion of the moment, he didn't remember how to turn it off either.

The following day, word spread over the community of how Josh had turned back the whole army of bandits with nothing but his crossbow. Some said there were a hundred of them. By the end of the day, the word was there were thousands.

Charlie Peterson, Ginger's dad, appeared unimpressed. Since he had kicked his daughter out of his house, he had refused to acknowledge she or Josh even existed. This was not easy to do in the small confines of the church where they both ate and worshiped. When either Josh or ginger was around, he would solemnly look the other way and there was no joy in him.

CHAPTER FOURTEEN

Ginger and Josh were honeymooning in the biggest house on the road. It was the one they merely claimed and hoped the original owner would never return. Josh kept busy all winter chopping wood, and supplementing their tofu allowance at the church with fish and game.

He was chopping wood for Larson as well. Most of the firewood he could gather was green or wet and hard to burn. Larson had a large pile of well seasoned wood, but was getting too old to keep himself supplied. The firewood Josh supplied was stacked out of the weather and left to season for the following year.

Larson shared his seasoned wood with Josh. For this, he let Josh use his chain saw and splitting maul. "Folks around here will only buy a Stihl or Husqvarna chain saw," he told Josh. All the other brands fall apart too quick. And use my Monster Maul for splitting. It beats anything else. Of course, you want to enjoy the chain saw while you have it. When you run out of oil for it, you will have to use an old fashioned buck saw."

Early on, Josh had made himself the crossbow. No sense in wasting ammunition using a gun. One cold morning he killed a rabbit and took it by to give to the Larson's. They were always glad to see him and appreciated the fresh meat he brought. This morning, Mrs. Larson treated him with a cup of hot chocolate. Josh marveled at how warm it was in the Larson house. "I envy you in your underground house," he said as he sat at the dining room table. "We enjoy our big house, but it is hard to keep clean and even harder to heat."

"It may not all be because we are earth sheltered," said Larson. "What kind of stove do you have over there?"

"Just a regular fireplace. We like to sit in front of the open fire on a cold winter evening and watch it burn."

"There is your problem, said Larson. "A fireplace sends most of the heat up the chimney. We have an up-to-date EPA approved catalytic wood stove. We extract energy even out of the smoke and pump most of the heat into the house. You may notice you don't see much smoke coming out of our chimney."

Folks up and down the road were building a commons building on the church property large enough to accommodate everyone in the community. They used parts of old barns for materials. It served as a dining and meeting hall, a tofu preparing kitchen, and grain mill.

Helen set up a clinic in the Larson's earth sheltered house where the temperature was never extreme and solar powered batteries provided some electricity for good lighting when needed.

Winter passed and the little community of Three-Mile road survived. Families put in a large garden. Larson gave classes on how to build solar food dryers.

Wild dandelions sent up a tangle of reddish leaves everywhere. People were up and down the road digging up the roots. They peeled them, sliced them, and boiled them with a little soda, then they boiled them again. With a little seasoning, they were a welcome change from tofu. They also ate the crown between the roots and the leaves. These proved tasty as greens until the plants blossomed.

As fruits and vegetables ripened, residents of THREE MILE ROAD brought their produce to market in near-by towns.

With the dollar worthless, barter was the order of the day and anything edible commanded the highest premium.

CHAPTER FIFTEEN

The story of Fred, Helen, and their son, Josh fleeing Dallas is told to dramatize the challenges we all may face in the coming months as the dollar loses all value and the late great USA sinks into chaos.

We carry an umbrella when it looks like rain. We carry insurance to cover our homes, our cars, our lives, lest disaster strikes. When we find ourselves facing an unsure future, we prepare ourselves for the hardships to come.

An old Chinese curse says, "May you be born in interesting times." A look at history shows few eras are without unique challenges. Hurricanes, tornadoes, floods, wild fires, earth quakes, volcanoes, tsunamis, civil unrest, wars, famines, and plagues are all too common. Empires crumble. Economies collapse. None of us are going to live forever, but it is the duty of each generation to pave the way for the next.

For starters, it is only prudent to prepare an evacuation kit and hope you never have to use it. Evacuate in an emergency early to avoid the congestion on the highway.

Here is the suggested list of items to have in an evacuation kit.

Three gallons of water for each evacuee. We can live three weeks without food, but only three days without water.

Mess kits, or plastic cups, plates and utensils

Emergency preparedness manual

Portable, battery-operated radio or TV and extra batteries.

Flashlight and extra batteries

Cash or traveler's checks, change

Non-electric can opener, utility knife

Fire extinguisher: small canister, ABC type

Tube tent, pliers, tape, compass, matches in a water proof container, aluminum foil, plastic storage containers, signal flare, paper, pencil, needles, thread, medicine dropper, shut-off wrench, tor turn off household gas and water, whistle, plastic sheeting, map of the area(for locating shelters.

SPECIAL ITEMS

Remember family members with special needs, such as infants and elderly or disabled persons.

FOR BABY, formula, diapers, bottles, pacifiers, powdered milk, medications.

FOR ADULTS

Heart and high blood pressure medication, insulin, prescription drugs, insulin, denture needs, contact lenses and supplies, extra eye glasses, hearing aid batteries.

IMPORTANT FAMILY DOCUMENTS

Keep these records in a waterproof, portable container.

Wills, insurance policies, contracts, deeds, stocks and bonds

Photo IDs, passports, social security cards, immunization records

Bank account numbers

Credit card account numbers and companies

Inventory of valuable household goods, important telephone numbers

Family records (birth, marriage, death certificates)

Photocopies of credit and identification cards

Army Navy stores stock surveyed military equipment. They also stock MREs military rations in individual containers that last well and will sustain a person short term. A case of twelve meals is not expensive.

A long term food storage plan may be the cheapest insurance money can buy.

Learning first aid, CPR, and survival skills make good sense.

Records show an armed citizenry discourages crime. Be armed, learn to use your weapons and hope you never have to use them.

In the present situation, consider getting out of the stock market and out of paper currency. Move to gold, silver, and things that might be useful when the electricity goes out. Seriously consider moving out of the city.

Live in the most energy efficient house you can afford.

Decide if solar power is right for you.

Get to know your neighbors as the Harveys and Larsons did in the story, build a network of support with family, neighbors, and friends.

Plant lots of fruit and nut trees and bushes.

Plant a garden. Learn what grows where you are. What works in East Texas will not work in west Texas or in Idaho. Stock up on seeds for a garden noting expiration dates on all supplies you purchase

During World war II, some families were separated and never able to find each other again. After the big hurricane hit New Orleans, people were able to reunite using the internet. There may not always be an internet. Or even electricity. Determine now where you will find each other again, perhaps at a small town far inland away from cities and military instillations.

You are not alone. Spirit will guide you if you listen.

Should you find it necessary to forage for wild plants for survival, be sure the plants are safe.

> The Department of the Army put out a book titled THE COMPLETE GUIDE TO EDIBLE WILD PLANTS. In it, gives a test to make sure a plant is not poisonous.

Test only one part of a potential plant at a time.

Separate the plant into its basic components – leaves, stems, roots, buds, and flowers.

Smell the food for strong or acrid odors. Remember, smell alone does not indicate a plant is edible or inedible.

Do not eat for 8 hours before starting the test.

Test for contact poisoning by placing a piece of the plant part you are testing on the inside of your elbow or wrist. Usually 15 minutes is enough time to allow for a reaction.

During the test period, take nothing by mouth, except purified water and the plant part you are testing.

Select a small portion of a single part and prepare it the way you plan to eat it.

Before placing the prepared plant part in your mouth, touch a small portion (a pinch) to the outer surface of your lip to test for burning or itching.

After 3 minutes, if there is no reaction on your lip, place the plant part on your tongue, holding it there for 15 minutes.

If there is no reaction, thoroughly chew a pinch and hold it in your mouth for 15 minutes. Do not swallow.

If no burning, itching, numbing, stinging, or other irritation occurs during the 15 minutes, swallow the food.

Wait 8 hours. If any ill effects occur during this period, induce vomiting and drink a lot of water.

If no ill effects occur, eat a quarter cup of the same plant part prepared the same way. Wait another 8 hours. If no ill effects occur, the plant part as prepared is safe for eating. "

Soy beans have sustained millions in Asia over the centuries. In a famine situation, learning to make tofu could make the difference.

. Anyone interested in producing the various soy products needs to get the BOOK OF TOFU as it goes beyond the scope of this work.

You may be eligible for tax credits for installing energy efficient equipment. WARhttp://www.energystar.gov/index.cfm?c=tax_credits.tx_index

In many areas, a wood stove would be invaluable. The following website will list EPA certified wood stoves and their efficiency ratings. http://www.epa.gpv/burnwise/

THE MOTHER EARTH NEWS GUIDE TO ENERGY SAVINGS gives a good introduction to subjects as easy energy improvements, emergency power options, small-scale wind power, solar space heating, solar hot water heaters, wood stoves, bio diesel, and more.

NUCLEAR

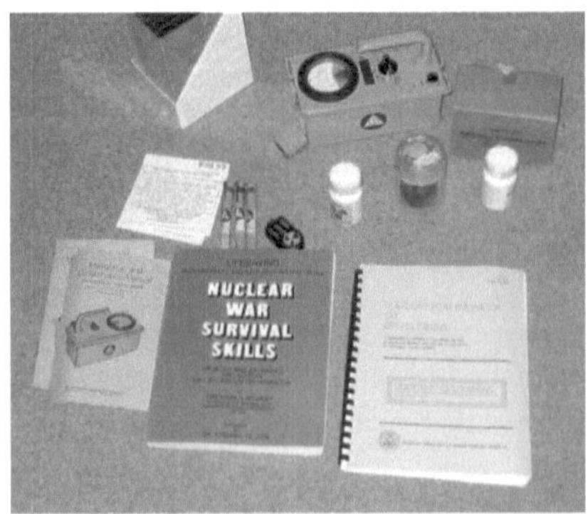

In the story of Three-Mile road, Larson's earth sheltered house would make a fine fallout shelter. The possibility of nuclear attack is more likely than ever before. The predictions of war are not far-fetched. Larson has the above pictured kit. A number of companies sell them. A quick search on the internet will lead one to them. Should you hear of a nuclear attack, you need to know if your area is affected by fallout and if so, where the safest shelter is, and when it is safe to venture out. The kit would be necessary to determine these things.

Something else to consider is. An EMP attack, (atomic bomb exploded high over the center of North America) would damage unprotected electronic devices from the Pacific to the Atlantic. It would destroy most exposed electrical equipment, plunging the country in the dark for decades. In a test, a relatively small high altitude, (about 240 miles up) blast knocked out street lights in Hawaii 800 miles away.

QUOTED ARTICLE IN AN IRANIAN MILITARY JOURNAL:

"Electronics to determine fate of future wars.

"The key to defeating the United States is EMP attack:

"Advanced information technology equipment exists which has a very high degree of efficiency in warfare. Among these we can refer to communication and information gathering satellites, pilotless planes, and the digital system…. Once you confuse the enemy communication network you can also disrupt the work of the enemy command and decision-making center. Even worse, today when you disable a country's military high command through disruption of communications you will, in effect, disrupt all the affairs of that country. If the world's industrial countries fail to devise effective ways to defend themselves against dangerous electronic assaults, then they will disintegrate within a few years…. American soldiers would not be able to find food to eat nor would they be able to fire a single shot."

The degree of your preparedness will be determined by what you can afford and how serious you are about preparing. There are many like Larson who move to the country for safety.

Can anything save us from chaos and a violent revolution? All things are possible through prayer but there is little time to build a consensus. We would need to go to our email correspondents, Tea Parties, to our churches, Lion's club, friends and neighbors and lift our prayer as one.

The Chinese symbol for “crisis” intertwines “danger” and “opportunity.” The immediate future looks sure to offer both.

SOME BOOKS FROM LARSON’S LIBRARY

THE BOOK OF TOFU by William shurtleff & Akiko Aoyagi

THE SOLAR FOOD DRYER by Eben fodor

THE COMPLETE GUIDE TO EDIBLE WILD PLANTS by Department of the Army

RAISING SMALLL LIVESTOCK by Jerome D. balanger

STALKING THE WILD ASPARAGUS by Euell gibbons

STALKING THE HEALTHFUL HERBS by Euell Gibbons

WILDERNESS MEDICINE by Dr. Basil spurling

ORGANIC GARDENING: NATURAL GARDENING FOR THE 21st CENTURY by Howard Garrett

MOTHER EARTH NEWS GUIDE TO ENERGY SAVINGS

YOUR CHICKIENS, A KID’S GUIDE TO RAISING AND SHOWING by Gail Damerow

COOKIN WITH HOME STORAGE by Peggy Layton

www.ingramcontent.com/pod-product-compliance
Ingram Content Group UK Ltd.
Pitfield, Milton Keynes, MK11 3LW, UK
UKHW041918190726
13854UKWH00003B/1319

9 781105 732065